The Halloween Visitor

Written by Michelle Smith
Illustrated by Tammie Lyon
Based on the character "Air Bud," created by Kevin DiCicco
Based on characters created by Robert Vince & Anna McRoberts

New York

Printed in the United States of America
First Edition 1 3 5 7 9 10 8 6 4 2
ISBN 978-1-4231-7171-3
G658-7729-415213
For more Disney Press fun, visit www.disneybooks.com

It was Halloween in Fernfield. The Buddies were admiring all the spooky decorations.

"Check it out, dudes," Mudbud said. "These jack-o'-lanterns are awesome!"

"Y-yeah," B-Dawg stammered. "Awesome."

Just then, a black cat dashed past the puppies.

"Ahhhh!" B-Dawg jumped.

"Dude, you're not scared of a *cat*, are you?" Mudbud asked B-Dawg.

"Yo, I wasn't scared," B-Dawg said. "But black cats are bad luck!"

Buddha shook his head. "Bad luck cannot affect a soul that has achieved inner peace," he said.

"Yeah. Besides, that's just a myth," Rosebud added.

"All this talk is making me hungry. Let's go get ready for some trick-or-treating!" Budderball exclaimed. All the pups headed home to get into their costumes.

Rosebud couldn't wait to put on her costume. Getting dressed up was her favorite thing about Halloween.

She was trotting by a shop when the same black cat scurried past.

"Silly B-Dawg," Rosebud said to herself. "How could he be scared of a cute little kitty?"

Just then, a cold wind blew down the street—and Rosebud was attacked by a plastic skeleton!

"Eek!" she cried. "You're totally messing up my hair!"

On his way home, Budderball stopped at an apple-bobbing booth that was set up at the Town Hall.

"Want to give it a go, Budderball?" Deputy Sniffer asked.

"Sure!" Budderball replied. A tasty snack was just what he was looking for!

Budderball dunked his face into the water. He came up with a shiny red apple in his mouth. Then he saw the black cat passing by.

"Hey, you!" Budderball blurted out, dropping the apple.

"Caw!" A big black crow dove down—and stole Budderball's apple!

By that time, Mudbud had
arrived home. There was a huge jack-o'-lantern in his front yard!
"Awesome!" he said.
Then he saw the black cat passing by.
"Hey!" Mudbud called with a friendly tail wag. "Welcome to Fernfield, dude!"

He tried to run toward the cat.

SPLAT! He slipped and fell right into the jack-o'-lantern!
"Oh, *no*," Mudbud said with a groan. He knew he was in for
something *really* scary now—a bath!

It was almost time to go trick-or-treating. Buddha put on his costume. Then he decided to center himself with a little yoga.

He was doing a complicated pose when the black cat ran by.

"*Namaste*, friend," Buddha said peacefully.

But suddenly, a fire truck drove by with blaring sirens!
"Oh, dear," Buddha said. "Now my chi is *totally* off."

When the Buddies were dressed in their costumes, they met up at the park. They all admitted that B-Dawg might have been right.

"Strange things happen when that black cat is around," Rosebud said with a shiver. "Maybe she *is* bad luck!"

"Shhh!" Buddha warned. "There's the black cat now!"

They hid and watched the cat hurry past.

"Let's follow her," Mudbud whispered.

"F-follow her?" B-Dawg whispered back. "Are you crazy?"

"Mudbud is right," Rosebud said.
"If this cat is bad luck, we need to warn
people. But first we need to find out
where she lives."

She ran after the cat. Mudbud and Buddha followed.

"Aren't we going trick-or-treating?" Budderball complained.
But he ran after the others.

"Man, this is wack!" B-Dawg exclaimed. "Wait for me!"

They followed the black cat up one street and down another.
Finally, she reached a deserted old shed at the edge of town.

She crawled in through a hole in a board.

The Buddies peeked in the window. "Here, kitty, kitty!" Budderball called.
"Shhh!" Buddha warned.

But it was too late—the cat had heard them. She dashed behind her bed of rags to hide from the puppies.

"Wh-what do you want?" she asked nervously.

"We won't hurt you, little dude," Mudbud said.

B-Dawg nodded. "Just stop giving us bad luck."

"Bad luck? Where?" The cat looked more frightened than ever.

"Guys, I think we were wrong," Rosebud said.

"What's your name?" Buddha asked the cat.

The cat shrugged. "I don't have a name. Nobody ever gave me one."

"You mean you don't have a kid of your own to feed you?" Budderball asked.

"Don't worry," Buddha said. "We'll find you a home."

The Buddies and their new friend headed back into town. Budderball sniffed the air. "I smell sweets," he said. "They must be inside that house!" He pointed to a big house with lots of scary decorations.

The Buddies and the cat walked up to the front door.
It suddenly swung open.
B-Dawg yelped. **"A witch!"**

But it was actually just a little girl dressed up as a witch. As soon as
she saw the cat without a name tag, she clapped her hands.

"I've always wanted a kitty," she cried. "I'll have to ask my parents,
but for now I'll call you Spooky!"

Spooky purred as the girl picked her up.

"I think Spooky likes her name," Rosebud whispered.

"Happy Halloween!"

B-Dawg cheered as he and the other Buddies
ran off to continue the Halloween fun!